PRAISE FOR *VERTIGO*

'Joanna Walsh's haunting and unforgettable stories enact a literal vertigo by probing the spaces between things . . . Her narrator approaches the suppressed state of panic coursing beneath things that are normally tamed by our blunted perceptions of ordinary life. *Vertigo* is an original and breathtaking book.'

Chris Kraus, author of *I Love Dick*

'Think Renata Adler's *Speedboat* with a faster engine . . . *Vertigo* reads with the exhilarating speed and concentrated force of a poetry collection. Each word seems carefully weighed and prodded for sound, taste, touch . . . The stories are delicate, but they leave a strong impression, a lasting sense of detachment colliding with feeling, a heady destabilization.'

Steph Cha, *Los Angeles Times*

'Her stories reveal a psychological landscape lightly spooked by loneliness, jealousy and alienation.'

Heidi Julavits, *The New York Times*

'*Vertigo* is a funny, absurd collection of stories.'

The Huffington Post

'Her writing sways between the tense and the absurd, as if it's hovering between this world and another . . . *Vertigo* may redistribute the possibilities of contemporary fiction, especially if it meets with the wider audience her work demands.'

Flavorwire, 33 Must-Read Books for Fall 2015

VERTIGO

Joanna Walsh

&other stories

HIGH WYCOMBE

First published in the UK in 2016 by
And Other Stories
High Wycombe, England
www.andotherstories.org

First published in the US in 2015 by Dorothy, a publishing project

Four of these stories first appeared in different form in *Fractals*, 3:AM Press, 2013.

The author would like to thank Lauren Elkin, Deborah Levy and Susan Tomaselli for support and advice.

ISBN 9781908276803
eBook ISBN 9781908276810

A catalogue record for this book is available from the British Library.

Typesetter: Tetragon, London; Typefaces: Linotype Swift Neue, Verlag; Cover Design: Hannah Naughton. Cover Image: 'At Sea' by Martin Brigden, used under CC BY 2.0.

Printed and bound by the CPI Group (UK) Ltd, Croydon, CR0 4YY.

This book was also supported using public funding by Arts Council England.

Supported using public funding by
**ARTS COUNCIL
ENGLAND**

CONTENTS

One of these stories is for E.
One is for F, one is for R, one is for L and one is for X.

FIN DE COLLECTION

A friend told me to buy a red dress in Paris because I am leaving my husband. The right teller can make any tale, the right dresser can make any dress. Listen to me carefully: I am not the right teller.

Even to be static in Saint-Germain requires money. The white stone hotels charge so much a night just to stay still. So much is displayed in the windows: so little bought and sold. The women of the quarter are all over forty and smell of new shoe-leather. I walk the streets with them. It is impossible to see what kind of woman could inhabit the dresses on display – but some do, some must.

We turn into Le Bon Marché, the women and I.

Le Bon Marché is divided into departments: fashion, food, home. It is possible to find yourself in the wrong department, but nothing bad can happen here. Le Bon Marché is always the same and always different, like those postcards where the Eiffel Tower is shown a hundred ways: in the sun, in fog, in sunsets, in snow. There are no postcards of the Eiffel Tower in the rain but it does rain in Paris, even in August, and when it does you can shelter in Le Bon Marché, running between the two ground-floor sections with one of its large orange bags suspended over your head (too short a dash to open an umbrella).

Fin de collection d'été. In Le Bon Marché it is already autumn. In 95-degree heat, we bury our faces in wool and corduroy. We long for frost, we who have waited so long for summer. In the *passerelle*, the walkway between the store's two buildings, a tape-loop breeze, the sound of water, photographs of a beach.

Je peux vous aider? the salesgirl asks the fat woman with angel's wings tattooed across her back. The woman mouths, *non*, and walks, with her thin companion, into the *passerelle*, suspended.

The first effect of abroad is strangeness. It makes me strange to myself. I experience a transfer, a transparency. I do not look like these women. I want to project these women's looks onto mine and with them all the history that has made these women look like themselves and not like me.

There is something about my face in the mirrors that catch it. Even at a distance it will never be right again, not even to a casual glance. Beauty: it's the upkeep that costs, that's what Balzac said, not the initial investment.

From time to time I change my mind and sell my clothes. I sell the striped ones and buy spotted ones. Then I sell the spotted ones and buy plaid. To change clothes is to take a plunge, to holiday. The thin girl in her checked jacket looks more appropriate than I do, though her clothes are cheaper. This makes me angry. How did her look slip by me? I was always too young. And now I am too old.

I cannot forgive her. I forgive only the beauties of past eras: the pasty flappers, the pointed New Lookers. They are no longer beautiful and cannot harm me now. Even your other women seemed tame until I saw the attention you paid them. I no longer know the value of anything. And if you do not see me, I am nothing. From the outside I look together. I forget that I am really no worse than anyone else. But how can I go on with nobody? And how, and when, and where can I be inflamed by your glance? I can't be friends with your friends. I can't go to dinner with you, don't even want to.

But why does the fat woman always travel with the thin woman? Why the one less beautiful with one more beautiful? Why do there have to be two women, one always better than the other?

Je peux vous aider?

Non.

There are no red dresses in Le Bon Marché. *It isn't the dress: it's the woman in the dress.* (Chanel. Or Yves Saint Laurent.) Parisiennes wear grey, summer and winter: they provide their own colour. *Elegance is refusal.* (Chanel. Or YSL. Or someone.) To leave empty-handed is a triumph.

In any case, come December the first wisps of lace and chiffon will appear and with them bottomless skies reflected blue in mirror swimming pools.

To other people, perhaps, I still look fresh: to people who have not yet seen this dress, these shoes, but to myself, to you, I can never re-present the glamour of a first glance.

To appear for the first time is magnificent.

VAGUES

There are many people in the oyster restaurant and they all have different relations to each other, which warrant small adjustments: they ask each other courteously whether they wouldn't prefer to sit in places in which they are not sitting, but in which the others would prefer them to sit. Sometimes entire parties get up and the suggested adjustments are made; sometimes they only half get up then sit down again. Some of the tables in the restaurant face the beach and have high stools along one side so that diners can see the sea. Others have high stools on both sides so that some diners face the sea and others, the restaurant, but both, each other's faces. Because of the angle of the sun and of the straw shades over the tables, the people who face the sea are also more likely to be in the shade. Not everyone can face the sea, not everyone can be in the shade.

The waitress passes. The people who face the sea cannot see her and cannot signal to her with their eyes. Facing the sea they can signal to nothing, as nothing on the beach can receive their signals, not the seagulls or the mother and toddler who are too far away, nor the occasional stork that picks through the rubbish. Yes, the beach has rubbish, though not much, and though the restaurant, by its presence, makes the rubbish unmentionable. All the beaches along this coast have some rubbish: either more or less than this beach. Here in the restaurant the diners who face the sea may notice it or ignore it, but they must accept the rubbish as part of the environment, just as they must accept the seaweed that covers the stones near the sea with a green slippery layer and which, unlike the rubbish, smells.

The smell of the seaweed must be accepted as part of the natural environment although it masks the scent of the oysters served at the bar, the smell of which is similar but different enough.

Farther along the beach, where the mother and toddler are paddling, the seaweed forms stripes of green that are pleasing, though this may be the effect of distance. The mother and toddler could have picked a better beach. Although all the beaches along this shore have some rubbish, some have less seaweed, and fewer stones. This beach is not good for paddling, but perhaps it is good for oysters. Yes, the seaweed the rubbish the smell the stones must all be part of the environment oysters prefer, which must be the reason the oyster restaurant is here, allowing the customers seated at the tables to look out at the beach and the sea and, looking, to understand that it must be the environment natural to oysters, and to approve.

Because he has chosen to sit at a table looking out at the sea, in order to see and approve the environment natural to oysters including the seaweed the rubbish the seagulls the stork the stones the mother and the toddler, he cannot signal to the waitress and it is because of this, or because she is insufficiently attentive, or because the oyster bar employs insufficient staff during the busy summer season, that the waitress does not arrive with his order.

He says,

'Maybe they will bring the entire order at once, though I would have thought they would bring the drinks first.'

He says,

'They do not have enough staff.'

They employ the number of staff they can afford to employ and serve at a pace at which the staff is capable of serving. The capacity is natural and proportionally correct. Il faut attendre.

He says,

'They have too many tables.'

We must also consider the number of staff the restaurant can afford to retain over the winter months, which we hope may remain steady although the population of the island must shrink by — what? — fifty — what? — seventy per cent — and during which the catch of oysters may remain the same or may increase because the winter months are more likely to contain the letter 'r', during which it is said oysters are best eaten, since during their spawning season, which is typically the months not containing the letter 'r', they become fatty, watery and soft, less flavourful than those harvested in the cooler, non-spawning months when the oysters are more desirable, lean and firm, with a bright seafood flavour, so that, although all the tables in the restaurant will not be filled in those winter months during which the population of the island shrinks by — what? — forty-five — what? — eighty per cent — we may hope that the number of serving staff employed by the restaurant will remain steady.

Theories:

· *During the off-months for the visitors, which are the on-months for the oysters, are the oysters packed in ice or tinned and shipped to Paris?*
· *During the off-months for the visitors, which are the on-months for the oysters, do the serving staff shuck shells?*

Or

· *During the off-months for the visitors, which are the on-months for the oysters, are the restaurant and the oysters abandoned, and the staff laid off?*

The waitress passes our table again. She does not stop.

He says, 'I think these are summer staff. They don't know what they're doing.'

In another country my husband may be sleeping with another woman. He may have decided, having the option, being for once in the same city as her, finally to sleep with the woman with whom I know he has considered sleeping, although he has not slept with her up to now. It is lunchtime. Where my husband is, it is not lunchtime yet. If my husband sleeps with the woman he will do so in the evening. As he has not yet done so, as he has not yet even begun to travel to the city where she lives, to which he is obliged to travel for work whether he sleeps with her or no, and as I am here in the oyster restaurant at lunchtime in another country, there is nothing I can do to prevent this.

The man sitting opposite me, looking out at the sea the seaweed the rubbish the seagulls the stork the stones, all of which I cannot see but which I know are behind me, does not want to wait for his oysters any longer. He has come here to relax but the oysters are too relaxed for him. He says, 'Do you want to leave?' He half gets up as though about to leave but does not.

He wants to punish someone for the oysters' slow pace. He wants to punish the waitress, who has not brought his order, by leaving. As he is facing the sea, he cannot signal to the waitress, so he wants to punish me by leaving. He does not leave. Because he does not leave, he wants to punish someone (the waitress? me?) by failing to enjoy his lunch.

Already he has asked the waitress several things. In the queue for tables he asked the waitress for a table although he was not yet at the front of the queue. When he asked, he did not ask her but he said, *Excusez-moi,* which means, *May I get through?*, then he asked, *Pardon?*, which means, *I'm sorry?*, then he made a noise that sounded French and indicated the tables with his hand. Then he asked, *Oui? Oui?*, which means, *Yes? Yes?* Then he asked me to ask the waitress for a table.

Each time a group of people passed along the path by the restaurant, on bikes or on foot, he looked at them anxiously in case they were able to join the queue, but be seated at a table before him. There are two entrances to the restaurant, both of which are visible from the door, and he watched both carefully to make sure no one bypassed the queue. When he arrived at the front of the queue, he made a false start toward a table, but the waitress did not respond. He did not repeat this movement so as not to abandon his position at the front of the queue. He stood squarely at the front of the queue so that no one could pass until another waitress arrived to give him a table.

He has made an enemy of the first waitress. She will enjoy serving her enemy. Perhaps he too will enjoy this combat. I do not enjoy combat with waiters and waitresses although I am now, by association, also her enemy.

Now he is here, seated at the table that looks out at the sea. It is the table he indicated, the table he desired, from which he can see the sea the beach the seagulls the stork the mother the stones the toddler the seaweed the rubbish and, at the other side of the table interrupting his view of all these things, me.

He says,

'I want to leave.'

He says,

'Do you want to leave?'

He gets up from the table.

He sits down at the table.

He stands up and walks from the table to the nearest door of the restaurant, during which time the waitress brings the drinks.

Though I am able in some part to share his anxiety about the table the drinks the oysters I find, because he is so angry, that I can face their delay with complete equanimity.

The tables are each made from a semi-circular length of half the trunk of a tree set on wooden trestles. The high stools are of brightly coloured powdered metal. Above the tables, the umbrellas of natural straw spell relaxation.

He is not keen to relax. He is keen to get on. He is already late for his next station of relaxation, for the beach, where we have an appointment to meet some friends of his at a strict hour. He is worrying that we will be late, that they will be anxious, that they, that he, will not be able to relax. He takes out his phone to check the time. We must be on time for the deckchair, the towel.

A speedboat drives directly at the restaurant from the sea, so directly that I can see neither its sides nor any perspective, only its prow and the foam it generates. On its prow sit two people, a man and a woman, perfectly tan in black surf suits, and for a long time it looks like the boat will not stop and will continue to drive toward the restaurant, arriving, unlike the people passing on the path on the other side of the restaurant by bike or on foot, through neither of the restaurant's doors but directly through the tables, bypassing the queue entirely.

He gets out his phone and checks the time again. About this time my husband must be leaving for the city that is home to the woman with whom he has been thinking of sleeping. As I know my husband is unlikely to tell me the truth about whether he sleeps with the woman or not – though he may choose either to tell me that he has, when he has not, or that he has not, when he has – I have taken the precaution of being here in the oyster restaurant with this man who may wish to sleep with me. As my husband knows that I know he is unlikely to tell me the truth about the woman with whom he will or will not have slept, so that, even if he tells me the truth, I will be unable to recognise whether or not he is being truthful, he must believe that if he sleeps with the woman, he will sleep with her entirely for his own pleasure. I, if I sleep with the man who is sitting opposite me at the restaurant, though I will not lie about whether I have slept with this man or not, will be unable to tell my husband anything he will accept as truthful, so must also, by consequence, make sure that, if I sleep with this man, it must be entirely for my own pleasure too.

The speedboat has turned and the people in it, revealed to be six in number, all uniformly and perfectly tan and black, are either on the boat or in the sea beside the boat and are, with no hurry, doing something or not doing something, perhaps mooring the boat so that they can come to the restaurant to eat oysters, or not mooring the boat but doing something else altogether.

They are slim and tan and their slowness has kept them slimmer and tanner than the people who wish immediately to be in the restaurant eating oysters.

He says, 'Perhaps they are mooring and are coming to the restaurant to eat.' At that moment, our oysters arrive and are eaten quickly.

All the time we have been at the restaurant there has been the sound of the waves quietly repeating. *Vagues,* I think, undulate: *on-du-ler.* The sound of the waves is pitched and modulated precisely so as not to intrude, distract, but so as to remain constantly audible:

    perfection.

VERTIGO

My daughter has made her first sacrifice to fashion. She has bought a short pink skirt with lace, which does not suit her and for which there is no suitable season or occasion. It will remain unworn, but beautiful. When she wears it, it stops being beautiful. When she takes it off, there it is, beautiful again. For this, she has given up her money.

This holiday was predicated upon spending as little as possible. That was the foremost requirement, beyond 'having a good time'. It would not be possible to have such a good time without the satisfaction of having spent so little and, besides, expensive pleasures would surely be less authentic. To sit on the docks after the all-night ferry, now that is something that cannot be bought. And it is easier to combine the pleasure of being very strict, very stern about getting to where we are going, with that of being slowed by the cheapest route, spending very little, except time.

We had come to spend some time here.

———

Vertigo is the sense that if I fall I will fall not toward the earth but into space. I sense no anchorage. I will pitch forward, outward and upward. It is worst driving up the mountain to the guest house, where the road turns rollercoasterward, only avoiding an unseen drop by a corner, skirting logs scaled like the tortoises glued by gravity to the road.

At the turn of the road, willing the world to continue a little space, there is a man, a woman and a child. They are not tourists: there are few here. From the outside, the man is greater than the woman, who is greater than the child. The child is brighter than the woman, who is brighter than the man. Of their insides we know nothing, because we cannot understand the words that turn those insides out. I grasp at words in this language with other languages I know, languages other than the one I mostly speak, as though one foreignness could solve another.

Apart from the ascents, it's the nights that are hard, under lead blankets. The dark leaves replay over the light, then night falls curtainwise. I say 'falls', weighted – nothing to stop it – outwards and upwards as well as down. No streetlights of course: no streets. Heat doesn't linger. Cold drops with (like) the dark.

Dinner? Only for the interruption of the boredom that replaces blank space in which I would usually make the family food, and which is now filled by drink. Beer first, not wine; I will get drunk more slowly. Drunk. Something that happens to you, like a glass of water, and that happens in the past tense, even as you are drunk in the present, as the action taken to provoke the state was taken in the past. You drink and then you are drunk. That's all there is to it. But I drink more slowly when I become used to bridging this space, like you. You do it every day.

I turn discreetly to take the last of the wine dregs filled with something like tea leaves.

The red lead blanket with white crosses, a disaster blanket. I like to have it near me.

———

People forget how far things are. When we returned in the evening, the owner of the guest house was disappointed that we did not walk to the limit of the ruin. At first we feel disappointing, but then we notice how old she is. She is tough, but she cannot have walked to the limit of the ruin, or not for a long time.

At the ruin, the light-coloured people do different things from the dark-coloured people. The light-coloured people sit in the debris of the ruin. They look, from there, at other buildings in the ruin. I cannot tell whether they are happy or not. Sometimes they take out a bottle of water some bread some tomatoes some salty sheep's cheese some crisps some olives, and spread these out beside them on the stones.

The dark-coloured people sit on plastic picnic chairs between the ruin and the hut. They do not enter the ruin; they do not look at the ruin. They work there. Sometimes they sit with things they are selling, sometimes with glasses of tea or (or, and) cigarettes. They do not eat, or if they do their food is on a plastic table, not balanced on a rock.

The light-coloured people wear light clothing that does not cover their bodies. The dark-coloured people wear dark clothing that covers their bodies entirely and sometimes also their heads. The dark-coloured people do not acknowledge the strangeness of the light-coloured people, in fact they do not acknowledge them at all but dwell by them as peaceably as by the sheep or cattle that also sit, and eat, in the ruin.

From the middle of the ruin a whisper can go anywhere.

We sit in the ruin, each reading a book, or three of us read out of four. Three different voices speak to us. We have taught the children to read again this week. Here, where there is no voice, apart from ours, they are desperate for any other. They will even sing to themselves, sometimes. The boy whistles. He makes his voice croak. He sings the same thing again, but breathing in. A bird echoes the first notes of Vivaldi.

I wish you hadn't told me about the stone. Of course I also wish it had been me. I had already dreamt of a piece of acanthus leaf, unobtrusive egg-and-whatever carving, a perfectly single pebble, pocketable among the ruins – but I'm not the one who found it. As I searched, my glance purposely turned to smaller stones, to twisted wood. The ground here has an air about it, a purpose: it focuses on the fallen. It's to do with vision, seeing straight. My eyes turned away from my mind's purpose – or toward it, which may also have been away from it. My mind does not tell me everything it thinks.

My mind thinks, furiously, *you must know I will have to leave you, will have to go with the children when they catch you, my duty to go, at the gate here, at the airport. You are a fool. You will risk yourself for it, the stone, and you do not belong to yourself. You will risk yourself selfishly, for you are also yourself-in-us.* My mother catastrophes in me. I hear her shrill: 'They will throw him into a dirty foreign prison!'

You will probably get away with it but I will know that you have risked all that.

The people working in the field beside the ruin come and go. We can see them because they wear dark colours: the men always at a distance, carrying something, the women, brighter and more complicated, stooping over by the buildings, sweeping or cleaning.

Would it matter if you took it? Would they ever miss that stone? The pillars are laid out in rows in their field hospital. In this section the stones have tumbled, are frozen, falling. When will they follow? They will choose their moment.

'Don't touch,' I tell the children. My mother says in me: 'Prison! They will fine you.' Out loud I say, 'THOUSANDS.' The children say, 'No, hundreds. They wouldn't charge that much.' They are right. I am as ridiculous as her, a fool indeed. My own children told me I must be wrong, and I was. I am ashamed to have thought anything so stupid, to have thought it without thinking, but there it is. I am a good cook, and I can keep the house clean. I have a job, even. But, sometimes I see no more than is in front of me. There are times I should just keep quiet. That's what the younger generation teaches me. They take the words out of my mouth, which I tasted for such a short time after I snatched them from the generation before. I'd thought the words were mine. My children have reminded me I was wrong.

The boy shouts wordlessly: 'O Tannenbaum' (or 'The Red Flag' if you prefer), 'The Blue Danube', Vivaldi's 'Spring'. He's heard them on the adverts.

The men who studied mothers and sons had daughters. Freud was a case in point. Did he study her? No, he pretended she had not occurred.

In any case love must be passed on with no return. Not even with feedback.

It is cruel to expect me to be both mother and daughter – such different expectations. My daughter tosses her hair. I see it from far away, as someone who does not know her will see it, a man. She is twelve years old. It is the same gesture she used at nine, at ten. One day it will become sexual. Is it yet? I don't know. Why am I frightened by this progress? It will happen. It must happen. And it happens in only one direction. She will gain power, but it is not much.

This is power with no balance. I can weigh nothing against it. She cannot stop becoming powerful. She is not powerful yet. When she becomes powerful, it is not a power she will know what to do with. There is not much that can be done with this power, not by its possessor.

Some women take power in a country by souveniring. I try to imitate them, look only for what I can buy, but my heart's not in it. The bargain is the thing to treasure: the leap of possession, of which the keepsake is only the echo. And maybe for you it has been the act of stealing. I can't tell you not to take the stone; it is so beautiful. Your eyes have allowed you to see it out of place already, on your desk perhaps, a shelf. Now, even if you put it back, it would not be where it was before. I have been tempted, seen one carving balanced on another behind the rope, about to fall – an acanthus leaf detaching from its finial – but I couldn't have taken it. Happy with a tourist's herded pleasures, really I'm helpless without you. Could I ask for anything more? Yes, but only what you don't see within these safe parameters, and secretly. To enjoy the smallest allowed thing, to take these pleasures privately – is this an act of rebellion?

It is something I can take away that you cannot.

We've been invited to transgress, in any case, continually: to cross inefficient barriers, to enter without paying, not to pay for the children, or to offer the smaller price for them because that was demanded last time.

How big is a find, anyway? Yours is pretty big. Other pieces that look like nothing may also be finds – pebbles with no carvings may be equally missing from the whole. And, if you leave it, someone else will take it, of course . . .

I say nothing. I think you take nothing. As we go, I think we leave: a lolly stick, some peanut shells. They will biodegrade.

———

In the car park of the ruin, no other tourists, only a man loading into his car brightly coloured squat plastic horses for children to ride. They are beautiful! Or not. On holiday it is so difficult to judge. Should the ornamentation on the fire hydrant be admired like the ornamentation on the finial? It is very similar. But is it authentic/typical of the region/linked to a social/political/cultural event/unique/historic, or is it found everywhere?

In the car, I drive, he speaks:

'What did you enjoy most?' he asks the children. They weigh only the things he suggests.

As for me, I enjoyed the people, ate them up. I do not say it; no one else saw me do it. There are three of them, now, farmwomen, stooping in the furrows behind the tractor, as though looking for dropped change. Then a man kneeling by his motorbike in a lay-by. Here no one will help. You have to fix it yourself, or push the bike a long way.

TUNA PREFABRIK homes rise up, pink as tinned salmon. The cliffs remain as unimaginable as a picture. The restaurant we passed said, OPEN ALL THE YEARS.

The drive up the mountain now consists of stretches of road that have been memorised, can be linked together, until almost every metre of the road is expected – and as it becomes expected vertigo decreases.

Last journey up. How much of my fear is put on? To give you some perspective, my teeth feel like cliffs to my tongue.

———

The man in the row of seats in front says, SHIT. He does not look or sound like the sort of man who says SHIT often, and I am shocked to hear the word come out in his pleasant sixty-year-old voice. He is arguing with the airline stewardess about exchange rates while paying for coffee. The stewardess says she will check the exchange rate for him. I do not know whether the exchange rate is SHIT, or the coffee.

The man's T-shirt. Khaki. Between the seats, a glimpse: across the back just by the neck, a small logo, LIFE IS GOOD.

She realised she was happy and it was terrible to be happy with anything so ordinary. It was like looking down from a height on nothing in particular, only the feeling of being able to see it all at once, and the feeling of falling, which was not falling, and the irritation at being provoked to that feeling by nothing in particular. She swatted it away but the happiness would not leave. She was surprised to find things went on just the same beside the happiness, which did nothing practical, like make the stewardess arrive sooner, or the children behave better.

A pregnant child passes along the plane. No, she is a woman. I am used to the coarse skin of those my own age. Even the very old begin to seem normal.

The stewardess. No, I am not hungry. I will deny it very quickly, almost as soon as I feel it, or rather as soon as I feel the not being hungry, which is not the same as feeling nothing. I will deny it out loud so I don't feel it, or rather so that I feel what I say – which is an absence, or rather an absence of the absence that is hunger: so that I *don't* feel the absence. And, no, I am not one of those women who has learnt how not to eat, only how not to want. And it is not food only.

She said when the children were small she was not happy, but the children had already escaped what they were, made away with the evidence. All she had left was the declaration. So why continue to be unhappy? It was almost impossible to be unhappy now. To hold onto the unhappiness would be absurd. But to let it go . . .

Children who are bigger than their parents are folded into the seats behind, their limbs bent in all the wrong directions, a padded girl (fifteen?) clutching a fat cushion decorated with the photo of a pug sitting on a drawing of a heart.

When she tried to brush the happiness away, it buzzed back around her. In her son's drawings she could see how complexity might develop and, from it, how the Book of Kells *was made, Icelandic woodcarvings, those tiles in the Blue Mosque. It seemed masculine, this pursuit of pattern, or she ascribed it to masculinity because it was something she did not do herself.*

Geological faults. From the plane we look down on things that would do us harm were we to encounter

36

them. *She felt no vertigo although she could have dropped a hairpin onto the canopy of cloud and it would have fallen through as though there had been nothing there, which there was not. On the other side of the window, ice particles kissed the glass, which was not glass but was made from the same material as her kitchen blender that broke, even though it was made from the same material as aircraft windows.*

The third person. There was no sign of this happiness on the outside, she knew. She was bored by this happiness that seemed out of place, impatient to get rid of it. The feeling was less pleasurable than she had imagined it might have been, less well-defined, and when she felt along its strings she found it was not easily traced or attached to the objects she thought it might have been attached to. Perhaps it was not attached to anything at all.

Could her husband have been the cause of her happiness? She thought of him but her thoughts refused to alight on one feature that might anchor that feeling. She tried the physical: his eyes, his forearms, his cock and balls . . . they all seemed much as they had been, she could think of any with equanimity. Perhaps it was something he did, some quality of mind? No, none of these.

How long does a thought take to form? Years sometimes. But how long to think it? And once thought it's impossible to go back. How long does it take to cross an hour? The plane crosses the map so slowly, though it goes at how-many-kilometres-per-second. The plane desires, as its passengers desire – hoping the lustre below might be the sea – to come to an end, but its desires draw it across the land only by inches.

If we were flying from Paris we would just have left. The flight would be short. *She tried to persuade herself to forget the hours of flight already passed, so it would be as though the plane had just left the runway, but it was impossible. Why was it impossible to forget what had happened, impossible to look at time only one way?*

Holidays are about returning, losing. You *should* come back lighter than you went. I know some people think different, collecting fat and souvenirs, but I have lost something. *Why was it important, this having to get back? She had forgotten already. The objects that returned with her would be happier, she knew, when she reached the end of her journey. The tweezers would return to a place in which they knew their place, or one of their many places. The clothes would fall back on their cycle of washing and ironing, would breathe a sigh of relief.*

When he gets up, something in his back pocket traces a square along the lines worn by his wallet. It may be his wallet; it may be the piece of stone. I do not ask. He does not volunteer. He withholds its power. I allow him to.

The land tips away from the plane. No vertigo. Too high.

And, after the third descent, the departure of the idea of anything bad happening.

YOUNG MOTHERS

It's not so much that we were young, because some of us were already old, old enough for grey hairs. It's more that our children had made us young. Already in the youth of our young motherhood our children had given birth to our function. We hardly knew we were born of them, before we were named: Connor's mum or Casey's mum but never Juliet, or Nell, or Amanda, not for years anyhow, by which time we had skipped the remains of adulthood and were only old.

But for a while we were young. You could tell because we acquired new things made from young materials. Our things were smooth, plastic, round-cornered, safe: clearly designed to be used by the very young. It was necessary that we did not hurt ourselves, we young mothers, though the temptation was so very great. We were needed, and the plastic things were needed so we mothers, who had become our own children, did not hurt ourselves. See how patiently we taught ourselves to use the new things. You could call it nurturing.

It had not started there, at our birth: our youth went further back. Pregnant, we already wore dresses for massive two-year-olds: flopping collars balancing our joke-shop bellies, stretchmarked with polka dots. After we were born into our new young motherhood our trousers sprouted many pockets for practicality. Khaki was good (grass-stains, tea-stains). You could put them through the rinser. Fleece was warm and stretchy for growing bodies. Shoes were flat for running, playing. Colours were bright, so our children did not lose us, so we could not lose each other, or ourselves, no matter how hard we tried.

See how we looked after our young selves, awarding ourselves little treats – cakes, glasses of juice or wine – never too much. If we noticed ourselves crying in a corner, we went to comfort ourselves. Sometimes we left ourselves alone to toughen up a little, but always with a watchful eye. Truly we were well cared for. Look how carefully we introduced ourselves to new environments: on our first day at playgroup we may have been reluctant, tearful even, to be herded together by virtue of situation and approximate age, but we remembered the manners we had taught ourselves: a good grounding. Seeing ourselves shyly approach each other we looked on with approval, breathed a sigh of relief.

Then we had to remember how to play.

We young mothers sang nursery rhymes. We had not sung in years. It came hard to us, sitting on the floor cross-legged in coloured tops and practical trousers, singing about crocodiles all together, toddlers flopped in our laps. We had nothing else to sing. You would have thought we could have invented, for this fresh generation, the newness it deserved. But we were tired.

You might have thought we could have done it, but we were so poor.

At the end of each day when our men came home we young mothers were already tired. We were younger than our children: the children that had birthed us. Our men wondered how they could be married to such children. Bedtime approached, and the men settled down to something adult on the television. We mothers were terrified, did not want to go once more into the interrupted dark. Distracted by noises, bewitched by things that sparkled, we lulled ourselves to sleep, overtired, tearful, telling ourselves tomorrow it would be OK.

In the playground the next day, we watched older mothers bring lunch boxes and spare sweaters to children who might not have wanted this kind of mothering. They made sure the kids were still kids. And the children, ignoring them politely, went on letting the mothers be mothers, for who knows what ends.

THE CHILDREN'S WARD

I have had some good times in this body, like right now, looking out of the window. Opposite the window is another window, and through that window, another. The window frames are dark brown and made, perhaps, of metal. They come in pairs, one frame inside another, the inner located in the top right corner of the outer. The smaller frame might open, but none of the windows is open. This might be because it is raining. Through the window opposite is a white wall with a door frame and, through that, a window that looks onto another white wall. Sometimes people pass between the brown frames and the white walls, and their colours look shabby.

Perhaps, walking along the corridor with the windows, the people who come and go can also see me through this window, sitting and not moving, my face toward them, with the back of a smaller head between me and my window, which they must see only as a shape blocking the lower part of my face. I realise that my body is enjoying looking out of the window, and that this is because it has not been asked to do anything for some time. It has been sitting here, constrained, not so much from coercion as politeness, while, inside it, I have been waiting. In the seat across from me, he is waiting. Though he is a child, the nursery-red plastic chairs we have both been given are too small even for him, and child us both further.

The nurses wear blue – the uniforms of attendants at petrol stations: blue polo shirts, loose blue slacks. Around their necks, ID on red ribbons. Each visits us alone. Each brings a clipboard. We fill in our details with erasable pen. Each nurse asks me questions. The questions are not for me. The questions are for him and, not so much from coercion as politeness, I repeat them until he answers.

'Are you an atheist?'

'I think I'm more of a pessimist.'

He is nine years old, and he is the oldest child here. At the table behind us a girl aged about five, with one eye placed halfway down her face, looks at her fingers, which are short and twisted toes. Her mother hands her a book about princesses. She pries at it, then walks away, her elbows pressed into her sides, a flightless bird. Far at the other side of the waiting room, a different girl aged about three vomits onto the floor. Then a buzzer sounds until a cleaner comes with a bottle of amnesia.

The person who brought our clipboard (a nurse? a consultant?) takes it back, wipes it clean and takes us away.

———

And now I am still sitting, waiting by his bed, which may or may not be appropriate, as he is not in the bed, and never was in it, so it may not be the right object at which to direct my waiting. The bed is in a cubicle whose walls are made of curtains decorated with pictures of teddy bears that sit at right angles to each other, never parallel to the horizontal. They remind us that the people in the ward are children, though these children do and say nothing childlike. The seat I am sitting on is a long narrow couch. It is decorated with pictures of dinosaurs, also at right angles. This seat makes me small again. My feet don't reach the ground. I cannot sit back against its back: my thighs are not long enough, because the couch is also a bed. Its smell is the same smell as new clothes

Joanna Walsh

shops: synthetic, sweet as a nut. There's something of the body about it, but only just: the body removed, perhaps.

The ward is hot, and there is always sound. Somebody's baby is wired up to beep. There is always light. The people who wait are all women. The nurses are women. So are the receptionists, the cleaners, and some of the doctors. I saw a man once but he left. You left me at the door on the ground floor, holding me by the elbow, that most reluctant handle. Did I not expect you to stay, or did I not want you to? Or was it that I wanted but knew it would not work. You left gladly enough, or, not gladly, but perhaps without feeling anything at all. You did not see the ward. You could not imagine all this. Text, you said. Text.

The women with babies have one-way conversations. They do not speak to each other, but then neither do I. One of them makes a screaming noise but softly, then laughs, then repeats a scream caught in the back of her throat, dragged across her tonsils. It is directed at her baby and the noise is a noise of love. She presses a button on a remote and, behind her, someone on the TV appears and says something that crackles. Is she listening with pleasure? It sounds like a crossed wire. It doesn't sound like fun.

What will compensate me for this wait, which is so much longer than the wait expected?

Will it be clotheschocolatebooks?

I could buy, say, a silk dress jacket blouse for the summer. I could look online to see if any garment meets my thought: that would occupy my mind, would it?

A nurse comes.

She tells me Charlotte will update me.

I do not know who Charlotte is. I do not ask. I could stop watching the bed in which there is nothing, and go, once again, to the information desk across the hall, where the woman wearing an apron with puppies has no information.

If Charlotte comes she will tell me.

If she tells me there will be no more words.

There will be no more words soon.

Get ready for it.

No more words ever now.

No more ever.

I don't dare to ask any more.

I wait. I watch the bed.

The baby wakes. It cries. It beeps.

I hope she's OK.

I hope we're OK. I hope we're all OK.

OK?

But Charlotte being not here to give the reply it goes unvoiced perhaps will always which is sentimental so I guard myself against it by labelling it as such when the toddler in the bed beside sits up and vomits blood into a cardboard bowl he has been holding on his knee for this purpose which makes me start to sweat. It makes my body start to part. In a moment I know it will no longer be with me. Sensible of it to want to get away. Good luck to you mate, I can hardly blame you. If Charlotte comes with her words comes to tell me it all went wrong how would my body know it? How long before the parts of my body realised, independently, that something was wrong and arrived, severally, at panic? Panic is a still thing. I have felt it before: each limb nerve organ coming into extreme alert unrelated to any other, ready for action, but who knows what action, as there is no action that could help here. Each part of my body knows, individually, what action it will take, but none of them are telling. I sit in the middle of them. I have no control. They seem to be ready to run in all directions. But without their cooperation I cannot run, cannot scream, so I sit still and I look quite meek. I know what this feels like. I have felt it before. I am waiting to feel it again.

To occupy my mind I could think wouldn't you through time backward to milk cereal first school-wear awww plasticine cookies wooden blocks whatever slippery tales someone dreamt up so feelings can be applied to the objects we passed between us but that would be wrong it hasn't been all sweetness no has it not the hitting biting swearing complaining and the downright lying all of which happens to more or less everyone if we're to be honest especially if there's something going wrong and not all on one side oh no not by any means. No if I'm to construct a hypothesis let's have one utterly other. I'll play a game or tell myself a story, which will kill a few minutes at any rate. Games are maths things, stories are not, or maybe they are. The name of my game (or my story) is, 'What would I do?' *If someone came for us, for instance, at night when I am in the house with the children but otherwise alone. This is not logical. There's no reason, from this person's perspective, why he shouldn't arrive in broad daylight when we are equally alone. And there is no reason that, if he arrived at night when we were not alone, well-equipped for murder as my fantasies allow him, we would have a significantly better chance of survival.*

He makes a noise downstairs, this person. What would he be doing in the kitchen? There's nothing to steal there. He should be searching for laptops. He should be in the living room checking out the widescreen TV. With what does he make his noises? With the tools in the bottom drawer of the kitchen cabinet. He wants them to break things open, he wants them to hurt us. There is nothing in my bedroom I can identify as any means of defence. There's nothing from which to construct a story about how I might defend myself. I rattle around in drawers for it, but still I cannot find it. I need the story to escape from one disaster into another, neither of which I can imagine. But why did he come without tools, without a weapon? Perhaps he is not the burglar I've planned for but a junkie, a drunk, a psycho. I am more comfortable with a drunk or a psycho: his passion, when I counter-attack, will answer mine.

What should I do then? First off let's take no action: not to alert him by switching on the light, by breathing. Not to alert him to his role by picking up something that could be used as a weapon. Not to alert him by being. The less I breathe, the more any audible breathing must be his: the less I move, the less any noise of movement must be mine. The less I make myself, the more he is, the more what I am becomes him. The more I allow him to come into being, the fewer defences I have, the fewer defences I desire. I wait. And I am getting impatient. Does this person find me, and my children, insufficient prey? That I, or my possessions, or my children, are not desired by this

*person is more or less unimaginable. I am trying to imagine
it, but failing. He will desire me, still, when no one else does.
Is he a comfort to me then? Perhaps there will be a time when
he will not come any more, but I don't believe it. If he is not
in the kitchen it may be necessary to search for him room by
room. If he is not in the house there is still the garden, the
shed. If none of these there is the street, the town, the rest of
the world. Wherever he is, he remains a certain distance from
me, and all his movements and intentions are relative to me
and always will be until he comes for me. I don't know when
he will come and whether, when he finally arrives, I shall be
surprised that he is real after all. There is a phone by my bed
but I will not use it. No police will cheat me of this encounter.*

Nevertheless I think I couldn't kill the anaesthetist,
who looked like a baker in his white tie-cap. Nor do I
think I could kill the surgeon, who looked like a banker
without his suit. When he went under they said, did I
want to kiss him? Or, not did I, but did mum. I looked
around for her but she wasn't there. I touched his leg
because I couldn't reach his arm. There were wires. I
didn't want them to think me heartless after all, but
did they imagine that was contact? They'd already
taken him out of his body. Sensible of him to get away
too. I have no idea if he is still in there. Couldn't they
see he had already gone?

I cannot make a body meet another body, not even to kill in thought. Try another story.

When this person leaves my kitchen and arrives, armed with my fantasies, at the very door of my room, which of my children would I save first: the vulnerable youngest or the one able to run? A friend who worked a summer as a lifeguard told me how they do it: identify those most likely to survive and save them first; let the baby sink to the bottom. They are told, he said, to be 'pragmatic'. We tell stories in which lifeguards heroically save the most hopeless people when all hope has gone. It seems that, all the time, we should have been telling a different story. I didn't tell my friend at the time, but this seemed wrong. It would not do for my story. His story would be a bad story, whether about a lifeguard, or about the person downstairs.

Can either of my children be saved? Could I, as saver, make a heroic decision that results in a positive outcome, or could I make a decision that results in a negative outcome but which remains heroic nonetheless? Or could I make a pragmatic decision that results in a positive but unheroic outcome, or a pragmatic decision that results in an optimum outcome and also makes a heroic story? What if the pragmatic decision turned out worse?

In another story I walk along the hospital corridor of the children's ward in which portholes wink at adult-eye level. The woman with the baby is in the parents' room, where tea and instant coffee are 'supplied by local freemasons'. The baby is not with her. She is crying or at least tears are coming out of her eyes but she is silent and also turning the pages of a gossip mag. I eat Rice Krispies from a plastic bowl with a cow on it, with a plastic spoon. I ask her if I can make her tea. She says no. One distress parallels the other. Or, no, how could it, or if it does, it is only for a moment, before each returns to the specifics of her own misery. I look out of the window, while the kettle takes its foreign time to boil, onto a central courtyard whose walls are white, and all down every wall are brown frames that answer only each other. At the bottom of this pit is a white roof. The tea I make tastes of soap.

Back in the ward, the baby is there. It beeps. The woman has returned. She is watching television. She watches baby programmes. It is too loud. Her baby is too small surely.

I sit on the couch beside the bed. My legs dangle. Above the bed dangle a machine's legs, waiting. The doors of the bedside cabinet look like saloon doors, but they do not swing open. Perhaps a troop of mice will come out, perhaps a miniature marching band.

And I have stopped breathing neither on the in nor the out breath, either of which would have been a bit showy, but in the middle of a breath so nobody would notice, just to see if time might stop and the people in the room might stop too in the middle of their activities, and I didn't even know I was doing it until I was about halfway to empty.

Then Charlotte comes, and all across her apron kittens kiss.

ONLINE

My husband met some women online and I found out.

His women were young, witty and charming, and they had good jobs – at least I ignored the women he had met online who were not young, witty and charming, and who did not have good jobs – and so I fell more in love with my husband, reflected as he was in the words of these universally young, witty and charming women.

I had neglected my husband.

Now I wanted him back.

So I tried to be as witty and charming as the women my husband had met online.

I tried to take an interest.

———

At breakfast, I said to him, 'How is your breakfast?'

He said to me, 'Fine, thanks.'

I said to him, 'What do you like for breakfast?'

(Having lived with him for a number of years, I already know what my husband likes for breakfast, and this is where the women online have the advantage of me: they do not yet know what my husband likes for breakfast and so they can ask him what he likes for breakfast and, in that way, begin a conversation.)

He did not answer my question.

So I tried to take an interest in what my husband was doing. I asked him, 'What are you going to do today?'

He said, 'I will strip old paint from the shed.'

(I already knew he planned to do this. But, again, that is where the women online have the advantage.)

I said, 'That's nice. Have a good strip.'

He did not respond to my jokey sexual innuendo.

Instead, my husband went outside to strip paint from the shed.

When he had gone I thought:

His women are the sum of all their qualities, not several but complete, massive, many-breasted, many-legged, multi-faceted, and I participate in these women. Some of his women have been chosen because they are a bit like me, some because they are unlike. He likes them. And he likes me. He likes me for being both unlike but like them. He likes them for being both like and unlike me. If I met them, I know I would like them, most of them, as we are all a little alike. Or at least I would not dislike them for being like, but unlike, me, and for him liking them not better but — although, and because, they are different — exactly the same amount as he likes me. We are all trapped behind the same glass. He can make us spin for his amusement and turn us to view any side. He is greater than the sum of our parts, though each part of them competes with me: their qualifications, and their legs, and their hairdos, and their cup sizes. And I compete with them, and some of my parts even outshine some of theirs, which are occasionally mediocre. But I cannot outshine them when they are added together.

After some time I went outside into the garden where my husband was stripping paint from the shed and said,

'Why didn't you tell me about the women online?' And he said, 'I did, when you asked me,' and I said, 'Why did you lie about how long you'd been talking to them?' and he said, 'I didn't.' And I said, 'I saw your emails and it's been going on for months. And I don't care what you've done,' I said, 'I just don't want you to lie to me about it,' and he said, 'I can't take this from you again. You have to let it go. You fucked someone. All I did was send a few messages. You have to let it go.'

And I said, 'I didn't lie about that. You lied about it. Just tell me you lied about it and I'll let it go.'

And he said,

'No.'

In the evenings, my husband listens to old vinyl. My husband says to his women, 'I *like* old vinyl,' and so they listen to some old vinyl for him.

'You remind me of Debbie Harry,' he tells one of his women, 'and you look like Belinda Carlisle. You make me think of Debbi Peterson (from The Bangles), and you look like Dale Bozzio.' My husband has a line and he follows it.

The line is flat. It is a line of enclosed screaming women. They are stretched into an eternity of dental floss you could wrap round the world a thousand times. It's not their breasts I can't cope with, nor their qualifications. It's not their Debbie Harry legs, their Dale Bozzio voices, it's the way they multiply, each by each other, exponentially: it's the digits.

My husband is a god, many-headed.

Because he has multiple women, he may have multiple aspects.

I want the same thing.

So I have practised myself by writing to him, although we live together. I have somehow assembled some words that, when seen through a glass screen, might look something like it could begin to be somebody. Now that I can read over what I might be, I think I know which parts are me and which belong to my husband's other women. I have become, perhaps, almost one complete person who could, perhaps, have a conversation.

And if I were to use these words to write to my husband while he, simultaneously, communicated with his other women, or while I communicated with other men, would the words we said to each other lose meaning, or would this render what he says to them just more of what he says to me, and what I say to them just more of what I say to him?

Are there only two sides of the glass to be on? And if I were able to skip over to the other side, would the view back look like old vinyl, his women, their voices trapped on a flat plane, damaged, heard underwater?

I think all this while standing in the doorway of our house, looking out into the garden at my husband stripping paint from the shed.

I say to him, 'Are you having a good strip?'

And he ignores my lame joke, so I say,

'How's it going?'

And he says, 'Fine.'
And I say, 'Can I get you a coffee?'
And he says, 'Yes.
Thanks.'

CLAUSTROPHOBIA

MINUS 1 YEAR

In the house of women, everyone is losing it.

First my daughter's piano teacher. Then my mother. Then her cleaner.

There's something about our uncontrol, no men to watch over us. What if it never stops?

MINUS 4 YEARS

The air, both inside and outside my mother's house, smells of fried meat. There is nothing we can do to get rid of it.

My mother returns to the kitchen, feels herself extend backward into her house. 'The yogurts,' she says. 'Someone has stacked them. Who has eaten one?' she says, to me, as though I should know – for, after her, am I not the woman here?

'Did you not grate any cheese at all?' she says to the empty grater, which is so clean. The grater does not answer. She means me. She had left the kitchen to me, while shopping, and I have made lunch for my brothers' wives and their daughters.

My mother says, 'We can have dinner for lunch, or dinner for dinner. What would you like?' If I eat dinner now, I won't have to eat it later. But I might. I *must* stop eating. But will I ever dare eat enough to want to stop? From the side I begin to look boxlike: a shelf of breasts, lifted by some contraption, then – down! – a waterfall. Since I've been here, I eat more, stealing spoons of cream, olives from the fridge, though she has so much and gives it freely. And I drink, though no one notices the evenings spent furious with alcohol. I buy the wine, that's not her department. She doesn't see how quick the bright ring creeps down the bottle. A pop of a cork the answer: dinner for lunch it is. Meanwhile, she is swearing because something has gone wrong with the soup, like it was life. And death.

My mother tidies the food away into her son's wife and their children, her long years' job of loading things into people. While my daughter cheerfully kicks me under the table, my mother helps my third brother's daughter to concentrate on what is in front of her, to stop concentrating on anything that is not in front of her, until there is only what is in front of her, and then there is not.

'It's nice,' my mother says.

The girl says, 'It doesn't *taste* nice.'

'There's lots more in there,' she says to my second sister-in-law's first child, who hands back her milk.

She means drink up. Nothing means what she says.

'It'll go to waste.'

I, meanwhile, cannot drink, my nose filled up with something. I can't drink but I can't breathe in either. Something rushes in to fill the gaps before the air.

My mother brings the cake out of the tin, measures it, knife hovering, turns to me.

'Would he like a larger slice?'

'Mum, I am not married any more.'

My mother takes off her wedding ring to do the washing-up. She does not take her apron off to eat. She washes; I dry. It occurs to me that I would perform this task so much better if I were not here while performing it. My mother, washing beside me, perhaps feels the same. The washing-up liquid smells of sweeties. It tells me that it is ginger and peach. It smells of something we should still be eating. This seems wrong: it should smell of something after, whatever it is that comes after. The dishwasher crunches like someone larruped in some half-hearted s&m session. The time spent cleaning up outweighs the time consuming. Then there is the cooking, the shopping . . .

My mother likes to keep things in. I prefer the feeling I have when the full fridge is relieved. I am anxious that we eat every bit (perhaps not the preserves, the condiments) before restocking. When called on by my mother to cook for her guests (which I am called-upon to do as, after her, am I not the woman here?), I am anxious to redistribute – especially – food I know diners have previously rejected: leftovers, anomalous items, boiled carrots, a spoonful of hot sauce, a single tinned apricot. I do this by introducing them into stews, pâtés and other dishes. These additions are not in the original recipes and sometimes they ruin a meal, though in ways the eaters can scarcely identify.

I am aware that I spoil things mostly for the sake of geometry.

'A vegetable marrow,' my mother says, already, 'for supper? Would you like it roasted and stuffed with nuts?' This is not a question.

I am a vegetarian; there is only ever one choice.

There is no answer to this, none expected. There is no 'no'.

But I am glad enough to be here, in the clean house where there is always the smell of food, in the midst of someone else's. Home is a rehearsal, by which I mean a *repetition* like in French: both what's behind the curtain and in front of it, a cherry cake studded with the same surprise on repeat. It confirms itself; it must confirm itself.

MINUS 3 YEARS

Returning, the house is still full of useful things she does not use: an antique hairbrush (that hair in it is probably Grandma's). What have we bought her, we, her children, her grandchildren? She has no more use for most things, but she likes the presents' outsides and, momentarily, what is inside.

There she is (the picture of my mother, young): what's to fault her? Me without the wide nose, without the unwieldy female fat. When I lived with her, I was fat, both times: as a teen, and then later. That way, she knew I could not move.

Upstairs my mother has hundreds of outfits. She has bought some new for the occasion. But will she wear them?

'You should wear what you want, Mum.'

'It's different if you have to go out with him saying "that old thing again".'

My father's pills are on his bedside table. Round, brown, shiny. At first I think: a jar of chocolate buttons, delicious in their sugar shells. I eat a square of chocolate just to keep from feeling hungry later. Here even for a weekend, I am getting fatter. I can feel it in my legs.

My father's pyjamas are on the bed, himself flattened, a steamroller joke. The scented sticks on the bedside table breathe urine and candy. The ceilings are low. If I take a breath, the air will be solid. My mother's magazines are on her bedside table. In them are women who had cancer but did not die. Now they are wearing sparkly dresses and frosted lipstick. They are interviewed, their faces shining. It is Christmas (although it is not Christmas).

'I was just saying,' my mother says, though what she says is something I do not remember her having said before, or not to me.

But, Mother, you're copying me: you got that new pair of shoes didn't you? Here you are on your eightieth birthday, shelling again your former self. Don't you know how hard I worked not to be the same as you?

Why do I sit here, paralysed on your made bed? I
could walk. This is the country, and that's what you
do in it. But there are no pavements on the bare road,
no footpaths across the fields, just ragged unofficial
tracks past signs for trespass. In the village, the fruit
dropping from the trees in every garden, the summer
owners no longer in residence. My mother doesn't
notice, lives inside, double-glazed, while outside everything is dying for our pleasure: the wheat, the birds,
the lambs – and new birds, and wheat and lambs will
replace them soon for our delight. But not the trees,
which live longer. Maybe we are their entertainment.

The night before the party, I cannot sleep in the
house. Not being able to breathe is to do with a room
where there are no corners. It happens at night when
I wake up again in the white room in the white bed
with the memory-foam mattress and white shutters
over the window, if there is a window, for, if there is,
it is too far away. It recedes, shows only a patch of sky,
is barred with white metal across its centre. The shut-
ter latch will not un-jam, however much it's shaken.
The door has shrunk to its keyhole. I must keep still
if it's not to shrink further. If I take a breath in here,
the air will be solid. It's not that I can't breathe, it's
just I have to make the choice: expand my chest,

contract it. In or out – what should I decide? If I make no decision I might die here. I must keep calm if I'm to get out. I am unconvinced things will be better outside but I put on a jacket, jeans, open the door. It is 2:18AM. It is quiet, and I am in the country. I can breathe, but only just.

'Did you speak to me then?' She asks me, even here. 'Did you say something?'

MINUS 2 YEARS

Heaven will be one of those shows where everyone from your childhood appears to replay the best time. You'll have to guess who they are, from their voices, or from their description of an incident, before they appear. There will be continuous anxiety. When you see them, they will have changed, though maybe not enough. I, for instance, am no longer fat. I forgot to stay fat. Now, my family cannot solve me. Meanwhile, my mother has grown round. It is as though her body had been added to my body, and then we were divided. If I'd had any courage I'd have been a fat woman for longer.

My sisters-in-law are here for the party, which I must not call a party. We meet from time to time to notice how each other has aged: that's family. I keep on rising up to you, but you preserve your distance: the years are like that. There are so many of you, and you are still just the way I thought I'd grow up, with all that was enviably grown-up about you: the lace tops with modesty inserts, and the spangles as if for nights out, the stiff hair, the cardigans grown over with a fungus of secondary sexual characteristics – bristling with embroidery and drooping with labial frills.

Now that I am thin you admire me, though you no longer like me. I am old, nearly as old as you are, and I know now that a woman is not her clothes: she's the body under the dress, or what someone could imagine her body to be. A man doesn't care about a dress's size or its designer, or whether it's real silk or not, though I guess these all go to make up something. I have learnt that even underneath I am replaceable. You could employ someone to be me and get just the same thing, maybe even better, if you had the money.

My sisters-in-law, you have all come, hungry, for my father's last show and, notwithstanding, I admire each one of you. My difficulty is in admiring your mother-in-law. She's nice but she's not my type. 'Did you see that show with the dog?' the sisters-in-law say to one another. 'When it . . . ' 'Oh my!' Depleted enough to show sympathy only for animals, they are eating chocolates from a bag decorated with anthropomorphised sweeties. Crunch. They take off their heavy bracelets before going to the buffet: clack.

It doesn't seem like a party without men. But here's my father, wheeled in on a kind of catering trolley! He is in a box, surrounded by something piped, perhaps cream, or duchesse potatoes, though it could be carnations. Silent as always, he is wearing a dark suit and looks almost as if he is still warm. Like a whole cooked salmon for Christmas or a wedding, his last helplessness is just one more thing. The sisters-in-law are delighted by this culinary feat. But – don't worry! – this is not the sort of food to consume, only to admire. Like a cardboard cake, the point is it looks like something might jump out at any minute. The sisters-in-law wait. They know very well that the box is not food, only cardboard and icing, but it is polite to act as though it were.

I think at one point I stopped breathing, or had my breath taken away. And I can't remember what happened to the box. After, there was no sign of the carnations. Helping my mother clear up, there was a stack of paper plates, of plastic forks, smeared with something dark and crumbly, and the residue of marsh-mallow, or was it mayonnaise?

Whatever happened, we put it under our belts. Perhaps they ate him, after all.

MINUS 5 YEARS

'I'm glad we went to the sea today,' you say, before we get there. You can see the sea from the car, but we have not got to it yet, and you are glad. Perhaps later you will not be glad, though maybe setting the seal of gladness on your first glimpse of the sea will have been enough to make you glad later, or to make your later lack of gladness hardly count.

When we get to the sea, it is flat, a continuation with the land that moves only a little. There is no breeze. From the sea to the land come yachters, fresh from practising a sport that takes up money and time. Some of them even need assistants who must be paid to have fun with them. I had thought the yachters would be beautiful but, no, they are old. It has taken them so long to pile up enough money and time to go yachting. The yachts are white and clean but their owners' faces are creased. The women wear jaunty Breton tops whose stripes are youthful. But up close one would see they are really quite old, with blonded hair and pinked lips, a fine joke.

So this is our last morning: such a relief to get over the final hump of our time together. Coming back to land I find I have forgotten parts of my body, not having had the leisure or the solitude to examine them. I do not know, for instance, if my legs are hairy, or whether my eyebrows need plucking. I do not know what my legs look like at all, there having been no mirror where we stayed this last weekend, except for the small mirror at head level fixed above the basin in the bathroom. There was no need even to have a mirror there. It's perfectly possible to brush your teeth or wash your face without a mirror, but imagine day after day going on with no knowledge of what you are cleaning, or whether anything ever gets clean.

When you made partner, Mother said to me, *you must be proud*. How could I be proud of something that was not my achievement but its inverse? Unless I am such a secondary part of you that when you eat, I taste it; when you urinate, I am empty. I've seen my father do this. I've heard him shout at her to pick up the telephone, as though she were his extra hand.

Something goes round and round in my head. I am frightened I will change my mind again, and it will be too late. I won't be able to go back. Although I can think of no reason I shouldn't change my mind, I know there is a rule somewhere that says I am not allowed.

I am frightened it is not worth the risk.

Nevertheless, this is our last morning.

0 YEARS/MONTHS/SECONDS

And when I came back from the funeral, I woke in the night not knowing if I were here or there, the white box of my mother's spare room overlaying my own bedroom, laying heavy on it, and on me, heavy with her, and with my father (though you'd think he'd have been the weightier) hardly at all.

Now I am working in my kitchen. The children are somewhere about, perhaps in the living room. They bump about the house; blind lumps of my flesh, detached. They will crawl into the larder and eat sugar, they will watch too much television. They carry out my most slovenly impulses, as though I had never educated myself out of them. There are noises on the other side of the wall: people having a sing-song, tinkering on the piano. It sounds like a party, or perhaps like someone listening to a party on TV. Sometimes there are noises: a woman shouting 'no!' and moaning, over the sound of a news broadcast. And that's when I hope it's TV, but I can't really tell. What I like about home now is the sound of all the machines going at once: the dishwasher, the washing machine, the dryer. White noise. That's why I work here, sitting in the kitchen, though I have a study. It helps if there's rain.

Despite the machines, or perhaps because of them, I feel some discontent. What will shift it? Would I like a drink of water, a cup of tea, a whisky? Would I like something to eat? The mother in me offers to self-satisfy, but is never self-satisfied.

Mothers do not ask questions. Mine did not ask me anything except to verify: do you have (what I told you to bring: your raincoat, the sugar, the sewing machine)? Would you like (what you know I have in mind already: an Irish stew, a visit to a stately home, a sugar bun)? I never said, *no, I would prefer a steak, to go to a club, a wafer biscuit, or really, nothing, nothing at all.* I seldom said, *no, I have brought: a sunhat, the pepper, a paper shredder.* I usually brought what I knew she would ask for, because she had already told me to bring it, and it was the object, not the question, that had to be met.

What would have happened if, one day, I had not?

I get the tin out of the cupboard, open it, and cut myself a slice of chocolate cake. My mother had a lifetime of making cake, and I have learnt from her. She always asked me if I wanted cakes. 'I live on my own now,' I said. She made them anyway. They sat in my cupboard for weeks before I scraped them into the bin. This cake is rich and dark. It crumbles like soil. It tastes a little like soil.

And here she is, surprisingly, or perhaps unsurprisingly, unearthly, less substantial than she ever was, being the one who made the cakes but seldom ate them: a minute on the lips, a lifetime on . . . well that hardly matters any more. Mother is where we put things we don't like. I *must* remember, I think, as always, to judge her less harshly this time.

But I am looking at her buttons, not her eyes. She has been talking for a while and it has been difficult for me to look at her eyes all that time. I'm not sure what she's saying. She might be talking about baking. Her buttons are white with a gold rim. There are five of them. This gives me more to look at. Her buttons glint but they do not look back.

Wait, Mum, I have a question.

I raise my hand.

What was I going to say again?

There is no bottom to the cake. I'm digging through the kind of soil that supports rhododendrons: it's that dark. There's a little ice-cream spoon shaped like a spade. I remember one from when I was a child, when a sundae looked like a mountain (though only, always, for the first time).

I cannot button her eyes.

I think we eat what we need. I could eat the whole earth if you broke it down into pieces, if the pieces were small enough. I read one woman ate the wall of her house: she didn't know why. 'My body calls for it,' she said.

THE BIG BLACK SNAKE

We saw it under the road, in a ditch beneath the road that stretched under the road from one side to the other. The road was not really a road; it was more of a path. The path was so narrow that it was more of a bridge. The ditch under the bridge was so shallow that perhaps it was only a hollow. The snake was in the hollow, thick and black as a bicycle tyre. We could not see its beginning, we could not see its end.

Its head was hidden in some grass or a hole on one side of the hollow, and its tail was hidden in a hole or some grass at the other side. The path stretched over the hollow, and it stretched over the snake. There were four of us. We were all together. We could not decide which was the front end of the snake, and which was the back.

———

The snake did not move, and we did not move. The sun was hot. We wanted to move out of the sun, to the other side of the hollow, but we did not want to cross the snake. We knew that there were poisonous snakes in this area, and we saw that the snake was so very big and black that it could only be one of the poisonous snakes. We knew all these things all together.

Nevertheless we crossed the hollow.

When we returned in the evening the woman who met us told us that the poisonous snakes in this area are thin and green, and that they will come upon you without your knowing, and that they do not lie in ditches in the sun, the size and colour of a thick bicycle tyre.

And we knew that this thing about the snake that we had known all together was wrong, even though we had known it all together, and it was one time that we had known something all together, all four of us at once, the same thing. Though perhaps we had also known at the same time that what we knew was most likely unlikely, and that we had also known that even a poisonous snake would most likely not be disturbed if we crossed the hollow, and we had known that the snake, being so big, was most likely the kind that did not rise up. But it had been important that we agreed about the snake, and it had been important that we did not have to say this, but that we had known it at that moment, each and all of us, the same thing. Or it had been important, at that moment, to think we did. And maybe that was what it was all about, after all.

AND AFTER . . .

Let it be autumn.

Let it be another town. Let the houses be low-rise, undistinguished, a mix of old and new. Let the doctor's surgery in a terraced side street be new sandbrick with a porthole window and double doors, and thick brightly coloured metal bars at waist height to steady the entering infirm.

Let the branches of chain stores in the high street be too small to carry the full range. Let their sales be undermined by charity shops selling just as good as new. Let there be other shops stocking nothing useful: handicrafts; overpriced children's clothes; holidays on window cards, faded; homemade homewares. Let these shops be unvisited and kept by old women still peering from doorways expecting their ideal customer. Let fashion be something heard of somewhere else.

Let there be back alleys for cycles hung-over with brambles, with cider cans in ditches. Let these back-ways be quicker ways but let no one question the cars. Let these ways snake along the back of allotments and supermarkets and H-block schools on the ring road. Let the ways snake under the ring road. Let dog walkers use them: let anglers use them, and junkies. Let these ways be deserted when the children are in school, except for the odd dog walker or angler or junkie. Let each wear his particular uniform. Let no angler or dog walker be mistaken for a junkie: let no junkie be mistaken for a dog walker or angler. Let anglers only occasionally walk dogs.

Let there be children and old people but few whose occupation is neither hope nor memory. Let there have been immigration at some point: enough to fill the convenience stores, the foreign restaurants, but let it be forgotten. Let the children be all in school, a breath held in, released at 3 o'clock across the park. Let the town's rhythm be unquestioned. Let me be single: no children, no family. Let me not fit in.

Let there be a college where art students dream of cities they do not leave for.

Let art for the old people be something colourful and, for the young people, something black. Let their art be always things. Let the colourful things appear sometimes in the windows of the shops that sell home-made homewares. Let the art students sometimes fill an empty shop lot with black things. Let the old people go right up to the windows of the empty shop lot and squint and frown.

Let there be a coffee shop next to a head shop where the art students hang out. Let the coffee shop serve bad coffee. Let it have only yesterday's news and the local papers (let small crimes occur, and let occasional larger crimes, on the outskirts of town beyond the ring road, be personally motivated, down to nothing more than bad marriages, bad upbringings). Let me sit in the coffee shop and, while drinking bad coffee, hear the rumour that someone famous was to come to town but that the visit was cancelled. Let the woman behind the counter shake her head, her towelled hand continuing to spiral in the persistently streaked glass.

HALF THE WORLD OVER

I. FITZROY

You look at your feet at the end of the bath. They are still quite plump and pink. You are waiting for the day blue veins will stick up from them, when a yellow knob will angle the joint of the big toe. That will be when you will have ended up. You have always wanted to be old. The rest, the unwrinkled plumpness, is a fake, a mere waiting.

You have travelled to a conference where you are lionised, though no one in this country seems to know your work. You are put up at an expensive hotel where you are sad to find there is a gym but no swimming pool.

Another disappointment: you wanted to buy your ex-husband a book signed by the keynote speaker, but it turns out she will not speak until after you have left. You spend your days working: panels, seminars, interviews. You have little free time.

In your hours of leisure no sooner do you go somewhere than you want to be somewhere else; no sooner are you sitting than you want to be walking; no sooner eating eggs than you want to be eating chocolate. Always you wish to be in two places at the same time, always you want to be connected. Here it does not seem possible.

In this city the streets are straight and cross each other at right angles. It is easy to find your way. The buildings are either very high or very low. The shops say what they are on their fronts, vans go by with signs like Tip Top Butchers, house numbers are prominently displayed.

People tell you to take the tram but the distances they describe do not seem far to you. You walk and you walk.

You shiver in your jacket and thin dress but you do not want to wear the other clothes you brought with you. You go into shops where the clothes do not suit you, but because you are not at home you do not mind – still you do not buy anything. You walk some more, and all the time you walk you think you should be sitting.

In the cafés you sit then shift chairs to get a better position, a new view. The girls here wear their hair in knots on the tops of their heads. This is just like everywhere else. It seems always to be time for break-fast. A man bends down to feed his chow a strip of bacon. Out of habit you order soup, the cheapest item on the menu. You return to the counter to ask for butter. You are always hungry, always a meal behind.

You cannot communicate with your children, your ex-husband. To be connected you must stand very near a wall of glass.

Outside the café a homeless man is shouting *What happened? What was it? Does anybody know? Can anybody explain it to me?* His face is bleeding. He cannot leave the circuit of these streets.

But you like being here. At the hotel, where there is a restaurant at which you cannot afford to eat but where there is also a bowl of free apples in the lobby, the women behind the desk address you in French. On the thirty-seventh floor you sleep on your usual side of the bed.

———

You walk out of town to a sea you have never seen before. You intend to reach down and touch it, which you have never done before, so when you return to your own country you can say you have touched it, but in the event it is too cold and smells of seaweed.

All around events are advertised for children: they have given up on the adults. They have given up on everything here that is old: age is accelerated in this young country by the sea. Salt rots the ironwork's optimistic balconies.

You intend to enjoy walking along the pier but it is not possible. No one sees that you did not touch the sea. No one sees that you did not enjoy your walk.

———

At the conference's closing party you ask the head of a television network to show you the river. It is midnight and he has stood talking with his arm around you all night, but when you ask about the river, he says he is married.

You mention a friend who once travelled here. When you say friend, say acquaintance, say how do you say ex-nearly-lover? You describe him and what he does without calling him any of this, hoping to see his reflection jump into your listeners' eyes.

A writer gives you a copy of his book, yellowed along the edges. There must be a stack of them at home.

The man in the café wipes his chow's mouth with a paper napkin. *What happened? Can anybody explain it to me?*

You become worried that the head of the television network might have thought you wanted him for his power and his money.

From the thirty-seventh floor at dusk you can see the lights going on below, snaking the gridded streets. And at dawn someone is swimming in a pool on a lower rooftop. Everything is so like what you would like New York to be like. Perhaps now you will delay going to New York in case it is not enough like this.

Tap, bath, toe. Soon you will be going away. You will not see the writer or the chow or the homeless man or the head of the television network again.

Luckily there are so very many new places in the world.

II. NOTRE DAME

Sitting in the café opposite, I am happy I am not one of the tourists flowing across the road to see the cathedral, but I am happy I can see them. They are wearing yellow trousers, emerald trousers, blue boots. They are wearing red heels; they are wearing turquoise flats. Having a limited amount of space in their airline suitcases, they have thought for a long time about what they would like to wear to see this place. They have thought about what the place would like to see them wearing, and what their fellow tourists would like to see them wearing and what I, sitting in this café, would like to see. And even if they discovered – as soon as they got here – that their clothes were wrong for the weather, the setting, the occasion, they're stuck with them and they're going to stick with them. The tourists are mostly women, or perhaps I don't notice the men, who wear shapeless beige pants, shapeless beige hats. The younger women are all dressed the same, in the current fashion. The older women are dressed either more primly or more provocatively than the younger women, but always in reaction to them.

The locals flow past the café and over the river in a stream of grey.

I came to this café because it is not the café across the street. This is not the café I would normally come to. The café across the street is better but there are advantages here. From this café I can see the beautiful people in the café across the street: sitting at that café, I could only be among them. As I sit at this café I develop a certain affection for the people here, which makes me feel I might have chosen this café after all. They are not so well-dressed as the people in the café across the street, and more of them smoke.

Their voices are more raucous, and especially their
laughter. Their hair is not so expensive and is stiffer
and comes in colours that are easily named.

I resemble neither the people in this café nor the
people in the café across the street.

Despite being worse than the café across the street,
this is not a cheap café, but I am getting good value.
What am I paying for? The view of the cathedral
(which is not so good from the better café)? Do the
tourists worsen the view? I don't think so. They make
me sure the view is a view, even though sometimes
they are in the way of it.

A few hours ago I was on a plane. I have time to
kill, too much time in the wrong place. The day has
stretched and I have baggy hours that should be taken
in, taken up. There is nothing to do with this time
but put some alcohol into it.

The tables in this café are close, very close. A man
sits down at the table next to me. I wonder whether
he is French, whether he is foreign, whether he is a
tourist. I also wonder whether I could say hello to him,
in French or in English, whether we would like each
other, whether we could sleep together. Two days ago
I was in a hotel that reached the sky: thirty-seventh
floor, half the world over. My spine is compressed after

the flight, my legs unwisely crossed. I have never felt like this before. It feels old.

The man, who is older than I am and not particularly attractive, orders some food in English. On the plane I ate things I had never eaten before, things I didn't particularly want to eat at times I didn't want to eat them. The more of the things I ate, the more I accepted them, and the more angry I became in the times between, when they did not appear.

I order. *Madame*, says the waiter, *Mademoiselle* (more of the Madame nowadays). I am careful to speak French with an English accent. It would be disrespectful to the waiter who wants to practise his English, to the foreign man at the next table, to show too much proficiency.

The man's order arrives quickly. It is a steak. Portions in this café are large; portions on the plane were small, but still I feel full. I can smell his steak. It is the steak I did not order, both for financial reasons and because I thought it might be too filling. He eats his steak quickly with no wine. I eat a croque-monsieur slowly with a glass of wine that is not the cheapest on the menu. I drink so the scum of things rises to the surface. I spent my money on wine: he spent his money on steak. Who got the best value? He takes a bottle of Coca-Cola out of his bag and, when the waiter goes away, takes surreptitious sips. Perhaps he is economising too.

The man with the steak looks at my legs, which gives me permission to look at the message he is typing into his mobile phone. I cannot see it as the glass reflects. I feel cheated.

I am tired and slightly drunk and still hungry. He is full of steak and Coca-Cola and, presumably, energy: enough energy to cross the road and walk up the steps inside the tower of the cathedral, which I have never entered.

In a few hours I will travel back to the airport to take another plane. Sitting here I am already waiting to wait. I have had so many last times here, it is impossible to tell whether this will really be the last. Time, when it is limited, is more beautiful. My wine tastes of smoke, incense. How can I leave this place? How can I stop watching the flow of tourists across the road? (Look! That one dropped something. It catches the light, shines! A valuable or just a cellophane wrapper? She does not notice, does not return to pick it up.) I drink my wine. I eat my bread, put Paris into my mouth endlessly. Look! Look at the bread, the wine, the tourists! I cannot stop looking at them.

The man at the next table takes a large, black camera from his bag and photographs what remains of his steak with a lens so long he can he barely fit it between himself and his plate. The camera makes a soft expensive click. As soon as I hear this I know I could never talk to him. He finishes quickly, and quickly asks for the check. He gets up from his table and leaves.

He has hidden the remaining part of his large steak under his napkin. Our tables are close, so close I can still smell the steak, so close I could reach across and take it, eat it.

It's the dry point of the year, and I've been waiting for an answer for some time.

No one's doing anything. There are not enough people left in town to eat all the fruit in the supermarkets. It piles up, ⅔ price, then ½ price, then finally returns to the back room on tall steel trollies.

The night I slept with him, it rained. He wore a shirt that, although we'd only met a couple of times before, I felt was unusual for him. He wore a jacket with a mend on the elbow that spiralled in concentric circles. Then in the morning he looked not as he had looked the night before, but as he had the other times we'd met, and he smelled slightly of cigarettes and furniture polish.

In bed he asked whether I wanted to do what I was doing every time I did it. As if he couldn't tell without, as though he'd checked himself and remembered some rule. And he laughed small and inward each time I said something to him, each time he said something to me. At the end he said, wow, like someone smacking his lips after a meal.

The next morning I told him I have children. And he said, oh, and he asked me their names, and that was all the mention of them, though the mention of them had been waiting, not insistently, all that time.

———

The river is at a high point now though the weather is finally hot.

D took me walking by the river. There are women it is dangerous to talk to. D is one of them. You try to tell her something and she starts telling you a story about yourself. Before you know it you are pinned, can't move. I wanted to tell D everything, including about him, but I didn't. Feeling the wet air suspended all around me, I closed myself down like windows before a storm. Afterwards, I'm glad I did.

I heard he was having a party. He arranged to meet me twice but cancelled both times. When he sent a message saying he could not meet me, his tense slipped. He said he'd really wanted to see me again. I'd feared it was too true. There'd been a point at which he'd wanted to see me, but it wasn't now.

He has invited my friend to his party, but not me, the friend of whom I said that I wondered that he didn't like her, not me: she is prettier. And he said, *oh the British and their blondes.*

He is not British. He is from elsewhere. His party is for a holiday from elsewhere. I thought he was not the sort to celebrate, but it seems he is. I haven't heard from him for a week, haven't seen him for almost a month now. My blonde friend, who is not British, will ask whether he will see me at the weekend. I will find out what is happening – perhaps. And maybe we will meet next week.

———

He is having another party. This time he has asked me. I'm wary. It was a general invite sent out to friends. The email came only an hour ago: there has been an age of strategy since then. How to reply?

I don't. But I go.

On my way to the party I expose myself to the point between work and social in which nothing can happen. The libraries have closed; the cafés have closed. The bars are open, but I don't feel like drinking;

the restaurants are open but I don't feel like eating — and I don't want to spend the money. Should I have a cocktail before the party, for courage? Or would I arrive with too much of its evidence on my lips, in my cheeks? Should I walk the streets (if it is not raining)? Could I read, write, in the corner of one of the big café-like bars, inconspicuously enough? Could I shift time from this moment to add to other times, times spent — speculatively — with him? With all the time I have, I could learn a language, I could read a book, I could write a book.

In the end I walk nowhere and the wind gets up and the rain starts and it is still too early to go to his party. It is colder than I thought it would be. I didn't know it could be so cold on a warm day.

I get drunk at the party. He doesn't talk to me. I go into the bedroom and his clothes explode from the wardrobe, violent with dry-cleaning bags. He'll be elsewhere soon. I know he doesn't mean to stay. Already, he's been gone a while.

———

Oh, there were nice times that summer, but they were attached to the wrong people: dashing through the rain with B, with whom I didn't want a relationship, although he did. He took my bracelet and said he could smell my perfume there, a medieval love token. I thought this over-elaborate but the sun shone and the rain at the same time and there were puddles that looked deep and reflected the sunwashed sky.

But that was in July when it rained. Now it's hot enough to stand outside pubs at night and although there are not enough people in town to eat all the fruit in the supermarkets, there are sometimes still parties.

It never hurts to ask (that's what he said to me). That's not true.

Sometimes it hurts to ask.

The difficulty is working out the right point in time. As he still hasn't answered my emails I have waited for him in various places hoping he might turn up.

Finally I saw him last night at a party and he ignored me until at last he took me aside and said he was *sort of seeing someone else*, and I said, *s'OK* and he shrugged and said, *that's how it goes*, and I shrugged and said, *that's how it goes*. And when he said it he was quite close to me and he was wearing the jacket he'd worn when we met with the mend at the elbow, and suddenly I felt I could reach out and grab the mend and pull him toward me and kiss him but that wasn't possible any more, even though I'd come to the party hoping he would be there and hoping it might have been. And I was wearing the jacket I had on when we met, and when we met it had been draped around my shoulders and every time you kissed me it had fallen off one shoulder and you'd reached your arm around me to pull it back on.

For tonight's party, I'd put a temporary tattoo of a spider on my wrist because I'd thought it would be fun.

Over by the windows, L was talking with his work junior, M, and he said, *you're my Dalston homegirl*, and she snarled, *yeah man*, because she wasn't: she was just younger than him and a woman and not white.

Then L said, *make me a rollie, M*.

And she rolled one for him, thin and black.

It was not a fun party.

We don't talk now but sometimes I still like to see whether you are online. I can see when you're there because next to your name on my screen there's the little green light. I have the same green light. It says, *available*.

At least I didn't create a fuss, make a scene. At least I didn't leave inelegantly.

Elegance is a function of failure. The elegant always know what it is to have failed. There is no need for elegance in success: success itself is enough. But elegance in failure is essential.

I left quietly and walked over the bridge to the station and it was not raining and nobody knew I had gone.

NEW YEAR'S DAY

New Year's Day on the sofa. I folded my life in on itself, seven times. The last few folds it only bent. I was surprised it was so bulky.

———

Last night I went to a New Year's Party where I met an Indian. I mean that's how he described himself – 'I am an Indian.' I talked to him for a long time. He seemed neither more nor less interesting than anyone else at the party, where I knew no one well and most people not at all. He told me he had once taught business studies but had now gone back to running a business.

Everyone at the party was so lovely. Everyone was so happy. Everyone's websites were now in colour with hand-drawn lettering. Everyone liked cooking and eating. Everyone didn't see why they shouldn't like – shoes! Everyone had taken pictures of themselves or had pictures of themselves taken in thrift-store clothing. Everyone agreed they should take time out for themselves. Everyone knew the difference between need and desire. Everyone made surprisingly snarky jokes. But then everyone laughed. Everyone smoked, or used to smoke, but everyone also, or instead, did — yoga. Everyone was younger than me, even those who were older. Or maybe it was the other way round. Everyone knew how to take their time. Everyone knew the value of real success, though everyone once worked for a flashy magazine or somesuch. Everyone knew how to say fuck. Everyone knew when to say, fuck it. Everyone wasn't hurting anyone. Everyone knew how to keep some distance. Everyone knew when to let it go. Everyone knew when to say enough is enough. Everyone enjoyed cake. Everyone had a secret tattoo. Anyone who didn't was keeping it secret. Everyone was surprised at some things. Other things were no surprise to anyone. Everyone knew there's a time and a place, though not for everything. Everyone knew what it was like to be in a bad place, which was not here, or now. Everyone liked looking at things that were pretty. I can still make things that are pretty, but I don't now, and, as for the things I made in the past, I don't even like to look at them any more.

———

You made yourself small on top of me, and I held myself still while you told me about the lovers you'd had while we were together. I held myself carefully because if I showed any reaction you would stop telling me. And then I would know no more than before.

I know you will buy me a drink.

I know you will take me out to dinner.

I do not know if you will tell me the truth again.

I can't exchange this trinket for any of the others.

Because you are practical, you will put me away into some part of your memory that is folded. You will put me into the past tense. You will not be concerned to resolve your thoughts about me. You will not want to know what I think of you. Your skin has many folds. You can put many memories away in them, one for each woman. You will live with me there all your life: a little canker that does no real harm, folded into your skin. You have even not put me away yet, as, here I am, back beside you. You snore and it sounds like a shower of change dropped on the pavement. Your snore interrupted my dream in which I had unsatisfactory sex with S's wife. It made her spill coins from her pockets, and then it woke me.

RELATIVITY

I am sitting here on the bus when I begin to wonder how it is my clothes have grown neater than my daughter's.

We are sitting at the front of the bus. My daughter did not want to, but I wanted to see out. The bus is driving toward the sunset. The driver pulls down a black plastic sunshade across the whole front window in which there is an open frame. The road ahead passes like a movie.

My pose is informal, legs folded under me on the seat, but I remain neat. However I try to shake this neatness, I cannot. I realise it is the neatness of my mother, who we are travelling to see.

My daughter, who has just become a teenager, sleeps on my shoulder. What I had she has now. Maybe.

I wear tight clothes, but tight clothes make me neater. If I wear loose clothes, my body flows out and pushes against them.

My daughter wears tight clothes too, but they do not contain her. She has not learnt yet how they can. Does she already feel the discomfort of her thighs spreading in her sausage jeans? Doesn't she already know it's wrong to have legs that look like this?

I lift mine and cross them.

They look better. But, still, I look neat.

Among other middle-aged women I don't look too neat, and this pleases me.

I am dressed for, what? For anything that might happen to me: keep it coming! I've learnt that it does. I am dressed for things that are not. I am not too sexy, not too casual, not too unassumingly unassuming. I do not look like I have made an effort, but I do look like I might have made an effort to look like I have not made an effort, which is only polite. And I will not fall over if required to run in my shoes.

My daughter is dressed for one of the many occasions she imagines could happen to her in tight jeans, bangles, a lace scarf and a T-shirt with a picture of a fashion model that says, WE GOT THE LOOK. I dressed like that once: hoop earrings, off-the-shoulder sweatshirt, leggings.

I cannot drive so we must take the bus between cities. The bus takes us through the outsides of cities, through yellow new estates of family-shaped houses. The people there have jobs you could put in a children's book. I'd always hoped to end up in one of these places where no one has ever been old.

The bus takes us through the market towns where the old people live, and where the property is prettier and less expensive than in the city we have left, or the city we are travelling to. Once I would have wanted to explore each shop on each high street, to discover local features even in the chain stores. I'd have wanted especially to investigate the charity shops, knowing that, among the second-hand pleated skirts and polyester blouses I would find . . . what? I would have visited once a week, twice, perhaps every lunch break from my children's book job, before I went home to my house on the new estate on the frayed outskirts of town. I would have visited the shops inconspicuously. I would not have talked to the women behind the tills. They would not have known where I came from. Each time I arrived, they would have beamed at a fresh customer. I would buy nothing, but I would not lose hope.

As it is I have packed wrongly. I know that now. I should have brought tights (it's cold). I should not have brought the new trousers that don't fit. I didn't bring anything else.

The bus enters a large town (or a small city) scattered with sponge-on-stick model trees. Sunset: the trees blur at the edges, change colour. From a distance they are solid, square: from close up, a net of branches.

The driver pulls up the shade with the plastic window revealing the whole road ahead, the game of framing gone. And my daughter, who has been sleeping on my shoulder, wakes up. She shifts and — vast, monumental in sleep — becomes tiny in movement.

I can see my mother and father waiting at the bus stop. They are very small. My mother is wearing a pastel blouse and pastel slacks and pastel canvas shoes. Her shades are mint, peach, lemon, blueberry, cream. She is dressed as she would like to see her granddaughter dressed: edibly. Still she looks formal, arranged, neat. She cannot shake it.

I cannot hear what she says to my father. She says, 'Forty-five, and she still has to take the bus.'

The bus stops and out get the sort of people who travel by bus between cities: students, old people — mainly women — and the middle-aged who cannot afford the train and who have never grown old enough to drive. Out we get, and away we go, the young, the old and the failed girls.

DROWNING

There is now very little in my mind.

On the beach in front of the village, which is no more than a stony strip, there are some adults but no children, who are all on the sandy beach opposite, and a gravelled path on a slip road that leads to the hotel. I am wearing only a bikini, but I want to see the hotel. I had not considered that I would have to wear a bikini while walking from the beach to the hotel. I am too old to look good in a bikini and I have not, across the years, paid enough attention to looking good in a bikini for me to look good in a bikini. But, even when young, I never paid enough attention to looking good in a bikini so age is perhaps not the most important factor. I must walk through the streets as though neither age nor attention paid are factors, as this is a holiday village and it is quite normal for women who do not look good in bikinis to walk through its streets. Why should I be any exception?

I also have no shoes. The tarmac is a warm body beneath my feet.

The hotel is beautiful, even more beautiful up close than it was from far away. It is white and on its facade its name, which is the name of the village, is a dusty blue. There are three rows of windows on the front, on each, shutters, the same faded blue as the sign I could read from the beach across the estuary, within each, white lace curtains, and along each storey a blue ironwork balcony that spans all three windows.

The menu of the hotel restaurant is exactly what it should be: not cheap enough to be disappointing, not expensive enough to be intimidating. And there are ways round: *menu du jour, prix fixe*. I cannot see the food or smell the food but, reading the menu, I know that the food will be good.

There is no one on the streets. It's like lunchtime, except it isn't lunchtime. I'm not sure what time it is or how long it took me to swim the channel. It is colder than it was on the other side of the estuary. In the harbour in front of the hotel, boats blink white: a *défi* – a challenge – to the ocean, which is dark. It is beginning to get dark – no, it's not getting dark yet, it just feels like it might soon.

From the jetty I can see the beach on the other side of the bay, which the sun still hits, but I cannot see what you are doing. I cannot see what the children are doing. On your beach, sometimes you choose to pay attention to the children, and feel worthy, and sometimes you choose to read a book, and feel interested, or engaged, or intelligent, or whatever, but, whichever you are doing, I know you will be having fun, because you do not worry that the children might be neglected. You never have to make the choice to neglect the children. For you to read your book is not to neglect the children because you know that if you do not pay attention to the children I will. I have the choice to pay attention to the children, which I may or may not find – but must give the pretence of finding – fun, or else the whole concept of fun, and the holiday itself, tips over. Or I have the choice to read a book. But I know that if I do not play with the children, you will not play with them, not unless you really find it fun. My choice to read my book necessarily involves the worry of the possibility of neglecting the children. While you read your book with the attention your lack of worry affords, information enters your brain making you more interested, or interesting, engaged or engaging, and intelligent, and so you become less like me, who, not lacking the worry about neglecting the children, does not become any of these. I can no longer see, from across the bay, which of these two things you have chosen to do. And this is why I swam the estuary.

The children are, in any case, now getting too old to receive the kind of attention you are not willing to give them. They are losing their last childish things, their shoes and clothes have become bigger until they are barely distinguishable from ours. We had more children – more than one I mean – to preserve this childishness, and also so as not to have to spend so much time together. Had we liked each other less we'd have had four, five. There's nothing like love's dilution to keep things in proportion.

At the end of the jetty, on my side of the estuary, a band is playing. Only children are dancing. The adults stare at the band as though music is something they had forgotten. It must be dispiriting to perform like this, afternoon after afternoon. One man nods the tune to his partner. She fails to pick it up. There are stalls selling snacks and other things, but no urgency in the queue for anything. Everyone has enough money, more than enough money for food, and no one is hungry.

There are hidden patterns in everything. I should be look-ing at the waitresses who come from somewhere else and who are not here for a holiday, for whom being here is only a step to being elsewhere. But I am not one of the waitresses. I am one of the holidaymakers, and, though my compatriots in fun disgust me I must not dismiss their feelings as unworthy by refusing to stay onside.

All holidays are nightmares: you save up all year and what do you find at the other end but someone else's house with all their own particular domestic nasties? They think you can't see where they haven't dusted; they think you can't see the cracked tiles, the mould stains on the wall behind the fridge. Not able to afford an anti-home, a hotel, we make do with a para-home, with someone else's cast-off furniture, with the unfash-ionable crockery, the cheap fill-ins from IKEA. By 'they', of course, I mean 'I'. We too have built an edifice from which no one wants anything but escape. It will fade, like the hotel, and people will wonder why we ever chose to build there. It will outlast us, likely, though there have been instances of women standing in the ruins of their former homes, strangely triumphant. We could abandon ours, but we're still mortgaged to it, and by the time it's paid we may have nowhere else to live, or any means by which to move on.

As an alternative, we look forward to the trapped repetition of shore, the unfamiliar house, the road between. Again and again we will flog fun from that exchange, or something we're willing to call fun, after which we will begin to hurtle toward something else — the Christmas holiday, the Easter holiday — never any rest. When we arrive we will find they add velocity to whatever drives us forward.

It's September next week, and summer's already turned its back. Already, the weather's stopped being accountable. There will be few more beautiful afternoons when we can turn outside from the spaces we have made, spaces that have become unbearable. Summer is a platform from which to think about the autumn. In summer, some men see more of their families than they do all year, others stay in town with colleagues, with women who cannot leave town . . . Sometimes, often, you do not holiday with us, or you leave early . . . work . . . How have I lived those times you left? In abeyance. I thought it would be freedom, without you: it is not. The thing that I have with you is pegged to different parts of my body. When I move, when you move, one of them tugs, and others slacken so I don't feel I am tied in those places, though I am.

In one month it will no longer feel like summer, and I do not want to go into the dark again.

I go back into the sea because there is nothing else to do. Or, there is, but I do not do it. When I reach the harbour there is a sign. It says, do not bathe, and do not swim the channel *à cause des* something, *des courants* etcetera, *à cause des bateaux*. I did not see a sign like this on the other side of the estuary. There is a ferry, though it doesn't go for hours. I have no money, but if I wait, if I tell the boatman my situation, I might persuade him to take me . . .The light of the lighthouse blinks, then the lights on the boats, one by one. I look out from under eyelids puffed by saltwater. I have seen harbours before – in Nice, in Marseilles – but none so narrow as this one, so difficult to get into or out of. I walk back to the beach and walk in to the sea. It is my choice.

Shall I tell you what it is like to drown? It is very calm and quiet. I step over from the blue to the ink-coloured water. I cannot see beneath me. I had never been afraid of the sea, had not understood people who were. That was because I had only seen its surface and had seen things that float on it, like boats and seagulls. The surface of the sea is round when viewed at eye level, like the horizon, like the earth. It tips, flat as a plate, each time I do, both hemispheres reorienting around me whatever my angle. The two hemispheres are unequal. The lower hemisphere is cold. I do not know what goes on there. It is vast, and in it is ninety per cent of my body, which is kicking. In the hemisphere above, in which things seem more varied – the sky, the land, the buildings, the people on the beach – is my head. Having made myself so very available I'm virtually concave, will I sink or swim? Depends which way up you place me. Pretend it's fiction. Pretend you are drowning. Or pretend not to be drowning, because maybe you are. Though it's difficult to tell, the outcome will be identical.

I say 'you'. Of course I mean 'me'.

Far away, a small motor-boat turns in my direction and although it is a very small boat and very far away I am unable to see anything above the underside of its prow which prompts the idea that there is no reason anyone on the boat could see my small dark head which I can hardly get above the level of the waves. Though the boat is small, it is big enough to kill me, if it does not see me. I tread water, going neither forward nor back . . . then there are a few moments.

There is the moment I think I will stop and wave so that the boat, steering toward me, is less likely to kill me, inattentively. But I do not, because I have already thought this will not work, and this thought has cost me some energy. Instead, I continue, for a moment, to tread water, knowing that though this may prevent me from going forward into the path of the boat, I will lose more energy. Then – partly because it is less risky, and partly because I cannot stop myself – I shout in a small voice: no! no!

The boat turns toward the shore. As my life now concerns only the circle of water around me, these moments recede quickly into the past. The boat turns toward the shore and the danger is years away. I was not the same person then, or I am not now. In front of me is the same struggle for life. The thing to do is to pretend the entirety of under-the-water is not happening, or is happening to someone else, or that – no – that the context in which it is happening is entirely different, or that each movement made cannot be made otherwise, or – even better – to put it out of my mind, to find it boring.

But if I died . . .

The salt meniscus that curves under my bottom lip: if it were to curve over, if it were to become what is inside as well as outside me. And that is all it is a matter of. The thought of drowning used to smell of chlorine. Now it smells of salt. Each death is specific. And the fear during death is nothing like the fear of death at other times. My fear is of this specific death.

I can see the people on the beach who are lying with their toes toward the water. They are not very far away, but they are not looking in the right direction to see my head. On my head is my mouth, which is above the waterline, and with which I could call to alert someone on the beach to my drowning. But my mouth is connected to my lungs, which, being below the waterline, are cold, and so constricted by the weight of water as to make the action of shouting difficult. If I stopped swimming to tread water enough to raise my head, if I inflated my lungs enough to call to them, I would no longer be able to pull against the current, and then the shouting would not be loud enough, not in the right language, and do no good, and, even if they are good people, and attentive, they may not be able to act in time. If I drown, whose fault will it be? The fault of the waves, the lack of a sign, the fear inspired by the sign, lack of sufficient muscle? Does it matter whose fault it is? But there is not much time to regret other people, their actions or inactions. Isn't drowning itself enough for one day?

Here we are, in the present, me in here and you, with the children, on the other side, two among others. We have got this far and we are not mad. We are not drunks or drug addicts (though perhaps we should be). We do not shout in the street, and when you stand next to us on the bus we do not smell bad. We are not murderers, or rapists, or paedophiles. We are adulterers probably in no more than thought. We do not take things without paying at the self-checkout tills in supermarkets. Some of us don't even jaywalk. We don't steal milk from other people's doorsteps, even when our own has gone; and if we see a cheap lost necklace in the street, we drape it over a nearby wall or post so it won't get crushed and so that the owner will be able to see it if she comes back that way to look for it.

Despite everything, we are good people, who can hardly live in this world that continues almost entirely at our expense. The best thing is to keep on moving arms and legs, and watch the waves, almost as though moving forward. In this way, despair turns quickly over to happiness, and back to despair again. And, if you reach the beach, walk back across it like everything is fine, toward your family who would not like to see the abyss you have just swum over.

Dear readers,

We rely on subscriptions from people like you to tell these other stories – the types of stories most publishers consider too risky to take on.

Our subscribers don't just make the books physically happen. They also help us approach booksellers, because we can demonstrate that our books already have readers and fans. And they give us the security to publish in line with our values, which are collaborative, imaginative and 'shamelessly literary'.

All of our subscribers:

- receive a first-edition copy of each of the books they subscribe to
- are thanked by name at the end of our subscriber-supported books
- receive little extras from us by way of thank you, for example: postcards created by our authors

BECOME A SUBSCRIBER, OR GIVE A SUBSCRIPTION TO A FRIEND

Visit andotherstories.org/subscribe to become part of an alternative approach to publishing.

Subscriptions are:

£20 for two books per year

£35 for four books per year

£50 for six books per year

OTHER WAYS TO GET INVOLVED

If you'd like to know about upcoming events and reading groups (our foreign-language reading groups help us choose books to publish, for example) you can:

- join the mailing list at: andotherstories.org/join-us
- follow us on Twitter: @andothertweets
- join us on Facebook: facebook.com/AndOtherStoriesBooks
- follow our blog: Ampersand

Current & Upcoming Books

Joanna Walsh is a writer and illustrator. Her writing has appeared in *Granta*, *The Stinging Fly*, *Gorse* and other magazines, and has been anthologised in Dalkey's *Best European Fiction 2015*, Salt's *Best British Short Stories 2014* and *2015* and elsewhere. A story collection, *Fractals*, was published in 2013, and her memoir *Hotel* was published in 2015. She writes literary and cultural criticism for *The Guardian*, the *New Statesman* and *The National*, is the fiction editor at *3:AM Magazine*, and created and runs the Twitter hashtag #readwomen, heralded by the *New York Times* as 'a rallying cry for equal treatment for women writers'.